W9-ANH-740

Bugs Bunny™
STORIES

Including *Bugs Bunny and the Health Hog,*
Bugs Bunny the Pioneer,
Bugs Bunny and the Pink Flamingos

A GOLDEN BOOK · NEW YORK
Western Publishing Company, Inc., Racine, Wisconsin 53404

Bugs Bunny and the Health Hog

After seven straight days of rain, Bugs Bunny
was getting bored just sitting around his burrow.
"I need to get some exercise," Bugs thought.
So he grabbed his galoshes and umbrella and
headed for town to join a health club.

"We're having a special sale this week," the man at the Hillsdale Health Club told Bugs. "Ask a friend to sign up with you and get an extra three months' membership free."

That sounded like a great deal to Bugs. He quickly set off to find his best buddy, Porky Pig.

"Eh, what's up Doc?" Bugs asked when he reached Porky's house. "You look a little down."

"I'm bored," said Porky. "It's this awful rain."

"I know just what you need," Bugs said. And he told Porky all about the health club.

Porky hesitated, but Bugs insisted. "You know, pal," Bugs said, "you've been looking even porkier than usual lately. You should lose a few pounds."

Finally Porky agreed to give it a try.

The next day the two friends signed up at the
health club. They started off with an aerobics class,
exercising to the beat of a jazzy dance tune. But
while everyone else struggled to keep up with the
instructor…

...Porky found his mind wandering.

After aerobics, they jumped into the pool. But while Bugs churned through the water like a speedy torpedo…

...Porky found his mind wandering again.

On the way home after their workout, though,
Porky had to admit that he felt surprisingly refreshed.
"This is just the beginning," Bugs said. "Believe
me, the more you work out, the better you'll feel."

Bugs soon began to regret those words.

Day by day Porky became more and more involved in exercising. He began arriving at the club earlier than Bugs, and leaving later. He didn't even take a break for lunch. Porky was too busy exercising to think about anything else.

Bugs felt sad—and lonely. He missed his friend.

SNACKS

One night Bugs heard a knock at his door. He
looked up and saw two little pink feet. "It's Porky!" he
thought hopefully.

But when he opened the door, he saw Porky's
girlfriend, Petunia Pig, standing there. She looked
upset.

"I need to talk to you," Petunia said to Bugs.

"Go ahead," Bugs urged. "I'm all ears."

"What have you done to Porky?" she said. "He told me you think he's too fat. Now he never wants to go out to dinner because he's on a diet. And he's usually too tired to go out at night. I hardly ever see him anymore. I miss him."

"I know," Bugs said guiltily. "I do, too. But don't worry. I'll fix this mess."

The next day Bugs saw Porky in the locker room. "I was wrong about you," Bugs said. "You *should* be plump. Like the old sayings go, 'Quick as a bunny,' 'Wise as an owl,' and, er, let's face it—'Fat as a pig'!

"You haven't been yourself since you joined this club," Bugs went on. "Soon I won't even be able to recognize you. Besides, I really miss you."

Porky shook his head doubtfully. "You're right, Bugs," he said. "I haven't been much of a friend. But you were right before, too. I *am* too fat. I promise to cut down on my workouts—just as soon as I lose a few more pounds. Okay?"

"Oh, Porky!" Bugs cried. "How can I convince you that you're fine just as you are?"

Then Bugs Bunny came up with a plan. The next morning he showed up at the club even earlier than Porky. He sneaked into the gym with a can of silver paint and changed the number on one of the weights from 10 to 20.

When Porky Pig arrived later and began pumping iron, he could hardly believe his progress.

"Look, Bugs," Porky cried. "Last week I couldn't get the ten-pound weight off the ground, and now I'm lifting twice that."

"Great," Bugs said. "Now you won't need to work out so much anymore."

Porky patted his tummy. "No," he said, "I may be getting stronger, but I'm still as fat as ever."

Bugs was discouraged—but he wouldn't give up!
He decided to swipe a pair of Porky's sweatpants
from his gym bag. He took them over to Petunia's
and asked her to let out the waistband.

"I hope this works," Bugs told Petunia

When Porky put on the sweatpants the next day, he noticed nothing wrong…until he started lifting his weights!

"Wow!" Bugs exclaimed. "You really have lost a lot of weight. Now you can stop dieting and exercising, and we can have some real fun."

"Oh, no," Porky said. "I'm still a little too fat."

That week the carnival came to town. Bugs asked
Porky to leave the club early and go over to the
fairground, but Porky didn't want to miss his
afternoon calisthenics class.

So Bugs went to the carnival alone. While passing
by the magic mirrors in the Fun House, he had a real
brainstorm.

Bright and early the next morning Bugs hung a
magic mirror on Porky's locker door. Then he slipped
out into the hall to see what would happen next.
When Porky opened his locker and took a look in
the mirror, he squealed at what he saw.

Bugs strolled over to Porky. "Eh, what's up Doc?"

"Look at what I've done to myself with all this silly dieting and exercising," cried Porky.

"There's nothing silly about exercising or dieting," said Bugs. "But you overdid it. You turned into a health hog, and there's nothing healthy about that!"

Porky looked so sad that Bugs knew he'd learned his lesson. He told Porky about the tricks he'd played.

"So I'm the same!" Porky said. "Let's celebrate!"
He called Petunia and asked her to join them at the
snack bar.

Bugs ordered carrot cake and carrot juice for
everyone.

"Here's to physical fitness—in moderation!"
Porky said, lifting his glass.

"And here's to friendship," Bugs added. He gave
his pal a big grin. And Petunia gave him a big hug.

Bugs Bunny the Pioneer

"Hey, Porky! Petunia!" Bugs Bunny called excitedly to his friends one summer day. He waved a copy of the *Cotton Tale News* at them. "Did you hear about the writing contest?"

Porky shook his head. "I haven't heard of any contest," he said.

"What contest?" asked Petunia.

"This one!" said Bugs. "The subject is 'My Camping Trip.' Whoever writes the best true camping story wins a backpack—and the winning story will be printed in the newspaper!"

"But we'd have to go camping first," said Petunia, "and we'd need to buy all sorts of equipment."

Bugs grew even more excited. "I've got an idea! Let's rough it! Let's go camping in the wilderness like pioneers! We'll do things the pioneers did—paddle a canoe, cook over an open fire, sing under the stars. I'll write a great story—'Bugs Bunny, Pioneer.' I'm sure to win!" he said smugly.

Porky whispered to Petunia, "Let's go with him.
We could enter the contest, too!"

Petunia nodded in agreement. "Maybe *our* stories
will get into the newspaper."

Just then Elmer Fudd drove up. "Hi, folks. How do you like my new van? It's got a sink, table, beds. I'm going camping, and I want to be weally comfy."

Petunia peeked inside the van. "It even has a TV!" she exclaimed.

"How about coming along?" Elmer suggested. "It'll be lots of fun!"

"Wonderful!" said Porky and Petunia.

"Hold it, Doc!" Bugs said, blocking the doorway. "I can't win the contest this way. Did the famous pioneers Lewis and Clark ride in a fancy van? No way! They paddled up the river in a *canoe*!"

Reluctantly Petunia said, "Thanks, anyway, Elmer. We're going to rough it with Bugs in the wilderness."

Elmer was disappointed. "What did that wascally wabbit talk you into?"

"So long, Doc!" said Bugs before Petunia could reply. "See you on the trail!"

It took a couple of days for Porky and Petunia to get everything ready for the trip.

Bugs made lists of things to take and things to leave behind. He was too busy planning things to do any work.

Finally Bugs and Porky and Petunia set off in their canoe. Bugs was too busy being a pioneer to paddle but not too busy to give orders to Petunia and Porky. "Stroke! Stroke!" he commanded. "You'll have to go faster if we're going to find a campsite before dark."

"It's hot!" Porky complained, wiping his forehead.

"My shoulder hurts," said Petunia.

Soon they came to a stretch of shallow, rocky rapids. "Everybody out," said Bugs. "It's too hard to paddle here. Carry the canoe across to the other side of the rapids."

"Oh, dear, this canoe is heavy!" Porky cried.

On the other side of the rapids, they got back into the canoe, and after more paddling, they came to a sandy clearing on the shore. "This is a perfect spot for our camp. Beach the boat," Bugs said.

Petunia and Porky dragged the boat onto the beach. "Time to put up the tent," Bugs ordered.

"Wow!" said Porky after he and Petunia put up the tent. "I'm tired. How did the pioneers survive all this work?"

"They were tough—like *us*," Bugs explained.

"Now, like pioneers, we'll have to hunt for food,"
said Bugs. "I brought some carrots, and I see some
wild onions back in that field. Why don't you two pick
them? Then we can have carrot and onion soup."

Bugs leaned against a tree and whittled a stick
while Porky and Petunia picked the onions, made a
fire, chopped the carrots, and cooked the soup. "How
I love the rugged life!" Bugs said happily.

The soup was delicious. Bugs, of course, took the biggest share. He patted his stomach. "Mmmm—that was yummy! After you two clean up, let's sit by the fire and relax. I'll play my guitar, and we'll sing under the stars."

While Bugs sang cowboy songs, Petunia and Porky dozed. They were too tired to keep their eyes open.
One by one, the stars disappeared. Then, suddenly, lightning zigzagged across the dark sky, and thunder rumbled fiercely. "A storm's coming! Get inside the tent!" shouted Bugs, leading the way.

The three campers raced into the tent. The wind
blew so hard that the tree branches touched the
ground! The earth fairly shook! Rain came down in
torrents! A mighty gust of wind tore through the tent,
and the tent collapsed!

"Save the canoe!" yelled Bugs as he disappeared into a warm, dry rabbit hole.

The gigantic waves were starting to pull the canoe into the river, but Porky and Petunia caught it just in time. They huddled all night beneath the overturned canoe to keep dry.

The next morning the sun was shining. Bugs
hopped out of his cozy rabbit hole, stretched his ears,
and looked around. "Being a pioneer is fun!" he
said. "What are you two whispering about?"

"You!" said Petunia. "You slept nice and warm, but
we're cold and tired."

"The canoe has a big hole in it, and we'll have to hike home," Porky said.

"Well, pack the tent and start hiking!" Bugs ordered.

"You've been boss for long enough," decided Petunia. "From now on, we'll give the orders. *You're* going to carry the tent!"

As they started down the road, Bugs groaned. "Hey, Doc, this tent is awfully heavy!"

Porky and Petunia smiled at each other.

They hiked for hours, and Bugs never stopped complaining. "Oh, my aching feet!" he moaned. "How much farther do we have to go?"

"Oh, only about ten miles," replied Porky cheerfully, as he and Petunia led the way.

Just then Elmer drove up in his van. "Boy, are we
glad to see you!" said Petunia.

"Hi!" said Elmer. "Did you get caught in the wain?
I kept dwy in my van."

"We sure *did* get caught in the rain," Porky
answered. "And we're tired of walking. Can we ride
home with you?"

"You bet!" Elmer opened the door, and Porky and
Petunia hopped in. "Coming, Bugs?" Elmer called.

Before Bugs could answer, Porky asked, "Would
Lewis and Clark ride in a van if they were only ten
miles from home?"

Bugs gulped as Porky quickly shut the van door. "Thanks, anyway, Doc," Bugs said to Elmer. "I'm going to walk."

So Bugs walked and walked and walked. When he was too tired to walk, he *crawled* the last half mile.

"It's not all that bad, Bugsy, old boy," he told himself. "You're seeing the country up close—like a real pioneer—and it'll make one humdinger of a story for the contest!"

**Bugs Bunny and the
Pink Flamingos**

Bugs Bunny was walking down the street, eating a carrot and singing a song.

"Springtime is here…" he sang, "the birdies are chirpin'…the flowers are bloomin'…"

"Hi, Bugs," said a voice. It was Elmer Fudd.

"What's up Doc?" Bugs asked Elmer. "Getting your vegetable garden ready for spring?"

Elmer sighed. "The birds keep eating up all the seeds."

"That's a shame," said Bugs.

Just then along came some of their friends.

Daffy was pushing a heavy lawn mower.

"Shouldn't you be doing that on the *grass*?" asked Bugs.

"I just got it fixed at the repair shop," said Daffy. "Now I have to go home and mow the lawn. I hate that job."

"I've got to plant these petunias," said Porky.
"They're my favorite flower," he added, smiling at
Petunia Pig. "But all that bending over wears me out."
"I hate to say it, pal," said Bugs, "but if you
exercised more, you'd bend over better."

"Well, I've got to get going," said Petunia. "My fence needs painting."

She looked at Bugs. "You're lucky you live in a rabbit hole," she said. "You don't have spring chores."

"Right!" said Porky and Daffy.

"Listen," said Bugs. "I have an idea. I could use a little pocket money. I'll go into the gardening business and do all your spring chores for you. What do you say?"

"I say *yes*!" said Petunia.

"Me too!" said Daffy and Porky.

"What about you, Elmer?" asked Bugs.

"No, thanks, Bugs," said Elmer. "I love taking care of my vegetable garden."

The next morning Bugs started his gardening business.

He planted Porky's flowers, and he watered them every day.

He painted Petunia's fence.

And he took good care of Daffy's lawn.

"You're doing such a great job, Bugs," said
Petunia. "You really have a green thumb."
"My grass never looked better," said Daffy.

"I wish I could say the same for my vegetable garden," said Elmer. "The birds are eating the seeds as fast as I plant them."

"Our picnics won't be the same without Elmer's corn on the cob," said Porky with a sigh.

"Or his carrots," said Bugs. "Don't forget about the carrots!"

That afternoon Bugs saw a sign outside the hardware store.

"Wow," he said, running inside. "Those plastic pink flamingos give me an idea!

"How many flamingos are left?" Bugs asked.

"Twenty," said the shopkeeper.

"Perfect!" said Bugs. "Five for Daffy, five for Porky, five for Petunia, and five for me." He paid for the birds and dashed to the door. "I'll be right back for them."

In a few minutes Bugs was back with Porky,
Petunia, and Daffy.
"Here," said Bugs, piling five flamingos into
Daffy's arms. "I want you to carry a few things for me.

"Hold out your arms, Porky," said Bugs.
"Five flamingos for you.

"And, Petunia," he added, "five for you."
"Aren't you going to carry some, Bugs?"
asked Petunia.

"Of course," said Bugs.
"Five for me. And I'll lead the way.

"Follow me," said Bugs. "It's only a few blocks from here."

"A few *blocks*?!" groaned Porky. "I don't think I can carry all this."

"Sure you can," said Bugs. "We'll be there before you know it."

"Watch out, Daffy," said Petunia. "You're poking me."

"Sorry," said Daffy, dropping a flamingo.

Porky bumped into Daffy, and more flamingos fell to the sidewalk.

"Don't worry," said Bugs. "It won't be long now."

Bugs stopped in front of Elmer's house.
"Hi," Elmer said. "What are you doing with all
those pink flamingos?"
"A good question," said Porky.
"No time for talk," said Bugs. "Follow me."
They lugged the birds behind Elmer's house.

"Start sticking the flamingos all over Elmer's
vegetable garden," said Bugs.

When they were finished, Elmer looked at his
yard. "This is pretty strange," he said.

"Now," said Bugs, "let's hide behind that tree."

As soon as they were out of sight they heard a loud chirping sound.

"Here they come!" cried Elmer. "Those awful birds are going to eat the seeds!"

As soon as the birds saw the flamingos they squawked in surprise and flew away.

"They've gone!" said Elmer. "The pink flamingos scared them!"

"Exactly what I thought would happen," said Bugs.

"Bugs," said Elmer, "I don't know how to thank you. You've saved my vegetable garden."

"Now we'll have corn on the cob for our picnics," said Porky.

"And carrots," said Bugs. "Don't *ever* forget the carrots!"